Ana
and the
Sea Star

R. Lynne Roelfs

Illustrated by Jamie Hogan

TILBURY HOUSE PUBLISHERS, THOMASTON, MAINE

The tide ran away and left quiet pools on the beach. The warm sand kissed Ana's feet as she danced from one pool to the next.

Ana stopped and gazed past her reflection.
"Papa, look," she said. "A star!"

Papa bent down for a closer look.

"Careful, Papa," Ana whispered.

Papa slid his hand under and lifted.
The star, with its five tapered arms, filled his palm.

"Did it fall from the sky?" Ana asked.

"No," Papa said. "This is a sea star, an echinoderm.
It's an animal that lives under the ocean waves.
But you can still make a wish if you like."

Ana stroked one of the sea star's bumpy arms with a gentle finger. "Pretty," she said. "My wish is to take the star home with us."

"But the sea star would die," Papa said.
"It needs the salt water of the sea to live."

Ana thought for a moment.
Then she said, "I wish to be
a mermaid and go with the
sea star to its home
under the waves."

Papa smiled and said, "That would be wonderful.
But you are a girl who lives on the land
and needs the air to breathe."

Gulls chattered in the sky over her head.
The salty breeze whispered in her ear.

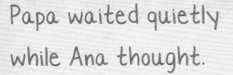

Papa waited quietly
while Ana thought.

"I want the sea star to live," Ana said.

Papa nodded.

Ana waited on the beach
where the waves tickled
her toes. Papa waded
into the water.

"Are you ready, Ana?" he called to her.

"Yes, Papa. Goodbye sea star."

Papa gave the star
back to the sea.

He returned to Ana on the beach.
Ana stared out at the waves.
"I still wish I could see the star's
home under the water."

Papa brushed her eyelids
with his fingertips.
"I will help you see it."

Ana closed her eyes.
Papa's voice was soft in her ear.

His words painted
pictures in her mind.

A loggerhead turtle paddled through the water with her big flippers. She didn't notice the sea star drifting by. She was swimming toward the familiar shore where she would dig her nest and lay her eggs.

The sea star fell . . .

. . . down, down . . .

. . . until it
bumped the sea floor.
It startled a stingray
burrowed in the sand.

The stingray rose
up and glided away
on silent wings.

The sea star waited as the sand settled around it. Then slowly, slowly, it crept home to the sea grass meadow on hundreds of tiny tube feet.

Ana opened her eyes and smiled up at Papa.
She slid her hand into his, and they walked down the beach.

"You made a good choice to send the sea star home,"
Papa said, squeezing her hand.

"Yes," said Ana, "but Mama won't get to see it."

"Maybe she will," Papa said. He winked at his little girl.

Ana watched a piping plover grab its dinner from the surf. The tiny bird skittered across the sand.

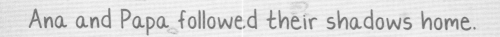

Ana and Papa followed their shadows home.

Ana let go of Papa's hand. The sea oats brushed her legs and whispered a welcome as she ran up the path calling, "Mama!"

"My girl!" Mama said, swinging Ana into her arms.
"Did you enjoy your walk on the beach with Papa?"

Ana nodded. "I saw a star and made a wish," she said.

"A star? During the day?" Mama said. "I wish I could have seen that."

Ana brushed Mama's eyelids with her fingertips. "Close your eyes. I will show you."

"If I close my eyes, I won't be able to see," Mama said.

Ana winked at Papa. "Just listen," she told Mama.
"I will help you see."

Then Ana painted pictures with her words
and made Mama's wish come true.

Hermit Crab

Unlike other crabs, hermit crabs don't have hard shells, or *exoskeletons.* Instead they protect themselves by inserting their soft abdomens into the shells of snails that have died. As they grow, the crabs must leave their borrowed shells for bigger ones, and they often fight each other for a shell of the right size—big enough to fit in, but not too big to drag around as they prowl along the bottom (usually at night) looking for food.

Jellyfish

Like hermit crabs, sea stars, and most other animals, jellyfish are *invertebrates,* which means that they have no backbone. Because they are not really fish (which *do* have a backbone), jellyfish are often called sea jellies. Their soft bodies are made mostly of water, and they use stinging cells on their tentacles to catch and eat the tiny, drifting animals known as *zooplankton,* most of which are smaller than the period at the end of this sentence. Jellyfish and sponges are the most ancient groups of animals on the planet.

Loggerhead Sea Turtle

Adult loggerhead sea turtles can weigh as much as 250 pounds (100 kilograms) and are about 3 feet (1 meter) long. Loggerheads are found in the Atlantic, Pacific, and Indian oceans, and the females travel great distances—navigating by the earth's magnetic field—to return to the beaches where they were hatched in order to lay their eggs. Loggerheads are an endangered species.

Sea Star

Scientists call starfish "sea stars" because, like jellyfish, they are invertebrates, not fish. They belong to a group of animals called *echinoderms,* which also includes sand dollars, sea urchins, and sea cucumbers. Most sea stars have five arms, but there are varieties with as many as forty. If a sea star loses an arm to a predator, it has the ability to grow a new one. A sea star creeps slowly across the sea bottom on hundreds of tube feet, which it can also use like suction cups to pry apart the shells of the mussels and clams it likes to eat. All it needs is a narrow gap between the shells; then the sea star protrudes its stomach through its mouth and digests its prey without swallowing it first!

Piping Plover

Piping plovers are small shorebirds that blend in with the beaches on which they feed. Their diet consists of tiny crustaceans, mollusks, and marine worms. The chicks can feed a few hours after hatching and can fly after about 30 days. Piping plovers fly south to the Gulf of Mexico, the Caribbean, and the Georgia and Florida coasts for the winter. They are a threatened species, but their numbers seem to be increasing thanks to efforts to protect their nesting sites.

Stingray

Stingrays are a group of fishes related to sharks. A stingray has a flat body and a long tail on which there is a spine with venom to ward off predators. Its mouth is on its bottom side, and it feeds on molluscs, crustaceans, and small fish that it finds by scent and touch on sandy, shallow bottoms. It buries itself in sand to hide while feeding, with only its eyes (which are on its top side) sticking up to watch for danger. You must be careful, when wading, not to step on a stingray!

Ana

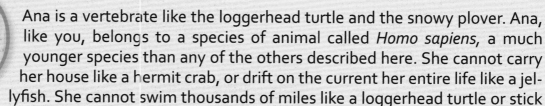

Ana is a vertebrate like the loggerhead turtle and the snowy plover. Ana, like you, belongs to a species of animal called *Homo sapiens*, a much younger species than any of the others described here. She cannot carry her house like a hermit crab, or drift on the current her entire life like a jellyfish. She cannot swim thousands of miles like a loggerhead turtle or stick her stomach out through her mouth like a sea star (at least we hope not!). She cannot flit through the air like a plover or soar through the water like a ray. But Ana, like you, can *imagine* all these things, and that is the most amazing power of all.

R. LYNNE ROELFS lives in Kansas with her husband and daughter. Sometimes she likes to close her eyes and imagine she's exploring tide pools on the beach. *Ana and the Sea Star* is her first picture book.

JAMIE HOGAN's award-winning children's books include *Rickshaw Girl*, which was named one of the Best 100 Books by the New York Public Library and won the Jane Addams Peace Association Award and the Maine Library Association's Lupine Award; and *Island Birthday*, which won the 2015 Lupine Award. Jamie lives on an island in Casco Bay, Maine, with her husband and daughter.

Tilbury House Publishers
12 Starr Street
Thomaston, Maine 04861
800-582-1899 • www.tilburyhouse.com

Text © 2017 by R. Lynne Roelfs
Illustrations © 2017 by Jamie Hogan

Hardcover ISBN 978-088448-522-3
eBook ISBN 978-9-88448-573-5

First hardcover printing October 2017

15 16 17 18 19 20 XXX 10 9 8 7 6 5 4 3 2 1

Library of Congress Control Number: 2017937850

Cover and interior designed by Frame25 Productions
Printed in China through Four Colour Print Group, Louisville, KY